Postman

and the Christmas Puddings

Story by **John Cunliffe**
Pictures by **Joan Hickson**

From the original Television designs by **Ivor Wood**

André Deutsch/Hippo Books

Published simultaneously in hardback by
André Deutsch Limited,
105-106 Great Russell Street, London WC1B 3LJ
and in paperpack by Hippo Books, Scholastic Publications Limited,
10 Earlham Street, London WC2 9RX in 1987

Reprinted 1988

Text copyright © 1987 John Cunliffe
Illustrations copyright © 1987 by André Deutsch Limited,
Scholastic Publications Limited
and Woodland Animations Limited

ISBN 0 233 98122 5 (hardback)
ISBN 0 590 70779 5 (paperback)

Made and printed in Belgium by Proost

Typeset in Plantin by Span Graphics

It was a bright day in November.

At the post-office, Mrs. Goggins said,

"Ted left a message from Granny

Dryden. She's run out of sugar, and

she says would you take a two-pound

bag when you call."

"Certainly," said Pat. "I hope she's

baking something nice."

Mrs. Goggins gave Pat a bag of sugar

with the letters, and off he went.

Pat called at Greendale Farm with
two letters and a parcel.
But Mrs. Pottage was busy.
She was very busy.
She said, "Put them on the dresser,
Pat. We're too busy to open them
just now."

The cooker was on.

Pans boiled on the hob.

The scales were out.

The mixing bowls were out.

The recipe book was open.

The table was full.

There were bags of flour, and sugar,
and raisins, and currants.

There were packets of dates, and peel,
and ground almonds.

There was a bowl of butter warming by the stove.

There was a bowl of brown eggs.

There was a small bottle of brandy.

Katy and Tom were helping.

They weighed the flour.

They beat the eggs.

They held the big wooden spoons, and stirred round and round in the big mixing bowls.

"My goodness," said Pat, "that smells good. Is it for a party?"

"No, it's for Christmas," said Katy.

"It's our Christmas pud," said Tom.

"Pudding," said Mrs. Pottage.

"And cake," said Katy.

"Lovely," said Pat, as he helped with an extra stir. "But what's that small bowl for?"

"That's your pudding," said Tom.

"Oh, it was a secret," said Katy.

"Never mind," said Pat, "I'll forget it before Christmas comes."

Mrs. Pottage put the puddings on to boil.

Tom scraped a bowl.

Katy licked a wooden spoon. She gave Pat the other one. They gave baby Paul a bowl to scrape, but he put it on his head!

Pat went on his way.

"Now, Jess," he said, "don't let me
forget Granny Dryden's sugar."

Pat called next on the Reverend
Timms.

The Reverend was in the kitchen, too,
with lots of pans boiling and
steaming.

"Are you busy with Christmas
puddings as well?" said Pat.

"Bless you, no," said the Reverend. "Miss Hubbard always makes me a lovely one. I could never eat two. No, I'm making grapefruit marmalade. Always comes in handy for church events, you know. Do have a jar for Christmas. It goes nicely on toast."

"Thank you very much," said Pat.

Pat was on his way.

At Thompson Ground, Alf was busy icing the Christmas cake.

"He does it better than me," said Dorothy.

Dorothy had already made the puddings, and she had two ready for Pat.

"Thank you," said Pat, as he went on his way.

"We'll have a lot of puddings by the time Christmas comes," said Pat to Jess, as they went along. "More than we can eat."

Jess would rather have fish any day, so he wasn't bothered.

Granny Dryden was always glad to see Pat, but she was specially glad to see him today.

"Did you bring the sugar?" was the first thing she said.

"Yes, I've brought it," said Pat. "It's been cakes and puddings all the way. It would have been hard to forget."

"Oh, that's lovely," said Granny Dryden. "You are a dear. I'll make you an extra pudding as a special 'thank you'."

"That's er . . . very kind of you," said Pat, wondering how many puddings that would make.

Even Ted was busy in the kitchen
when Pat called.
He had a big machine on the table.

It was whizzing and whirring like a
cement-mixer.

"Whatever is that?" said Pat.

"It's the Doctor's food-mixer," said Ted. "I've been putting a new motor in it. I'm trying it out on my mum's favourite recipe for . . ."

"I can guess," said Pat. "Don't tell me . . . I bet it's for Christmas pudding."

"You're right!" said Ted. "How did you guess?"

"I can see into the future," said Pat.

"There's just one catch," said Ted.

"You see, it's a big mixer, and it only works with large amounts. I think I've mixed enough for about ten Christmas puddings."

"Oh dear," said Pat.

"Anyway, I'll keep three for you. You'll easily manage three, won't you?"

"Well," said Pat, "I can't . . ."

"I know you like Christmas pudding," said Ted, "so don't be shy about having three. They'll be gone in no time."

And Pat didn't have the heart to say "No".

When Pat called on Miss Hubbard he was glad to see that she was busy making blackberry wine. There were no puddings in sight. When she said, "I've kept a special bottle of Christmas wine for you, Pat," he was really pleased.

BLACCK
BERRRY
NOOV

But when she opened the cupboard and took out a fat round packet, and said, "And a real home-made pudding to go with it," poor Pat almost fainted.

He said, in a wobbly voice, "Th...thank y...you very much, Miss H-H-Hubbard."

By the end of the week, Pat had
collected ten Christmas puddings in
the back of his van.

"Oh, Jess," he said, "all these
puddings! They're just too much for
me. I don't think I could eat even one
now."

I don't know what would have
happened to all those puddings if Pat
hadn't had a broken spring on the
van.

He had to take his van into Pencaster
to get it mended.

He did some Christmas shopping whilst he waited for it. There was a Christmas tree in the market-place. Some people were collecting for homeless families.

Pat put some money in the collecting box, and the man said, "Thanks. That'll be a good help for the Christmas Dinner."

"Did you say Christmas Dinner?" said Pat. "Is that what you're collecting for?"

"It certainly is," said the man.

"Would you like some lovely home-made puddings?" said Pat. "Ten of them?"

"Great!" said the man. "Just what we need. Great! Thanks!"

In the end, Pat put his name down to help with the dinner.

Everyone loved the puddings, and ate them up to the last morsel.

When Christmas was over, and Pat's friends said, "And how was the pudding?" Pat could truly say, "Delicious! Really delicious." I wonder if he'll get ten next year?